AF580620

Turtleberry Press

Baltimore, MD 21234

www.turtleberrypress.com

Keya has had a crush on her line sister Chantay for years. With the assistance of her best friend, she comments on a picture Chantay shared. Emojis were exchanged. Then Keya shares a sexy picture and it's Chantay's turn to comment. That leads to a video chat and next thing Keya knows she is sharing a room with Chantay on vacation. What could go right?

“Fuck, she looks good.” I chewed on my lip while looking at the new picture that Chantay had just posted.

“Lemme see.” Tiffany leaned over and looked at my phone. Then she looked at me. “I’ve seen her before.”

“She’s one of my line sisters.”

“I thought she looked familiar.” Tiffany paused. “I didn’t think she would be your type.”

“Why?”

“You’re both girlie.”

I laughed. “I like girlie.”

Tiffany nodded. “I’m glad that you’re embracing it.”

I looked back at Chantay’s picture and sighed. I was thankful for whoever took the full body shot of her at the harbor. She was wearing the hell out of her short red dress. Her dark brown skin looked perfect. “She looks the same as she did in college.”

“Keya, so do you. I’ve seen the pictures.” Tiffany sat her phone down. “Just go ahead and like the picture. You’re a girl so you can get away with flirting in the comments.”

“I’m not going to flirt in the comments.” After one last look at the picture, I liked it and then kept scrolling.

“You should have said something.”

"Like what?"

"Like whatever you would like someone to say about a picture you post."

"I guess."

"Scroll back and comment. It's clear you have a crush on her. Say something to make her smile."

"I'd rather comment on her story. Then it's not public."

"You're no fun." Tiffany rolled her eyes. "When's the last time you spoke to her?"

"We're in a group chat together."

"No. When's the last time you had a private conversation with her?"

"Oh, it's been a while."

“If you’re going to say something privately you need to say something worth the privacy.”

“Why can’t I just respond with a heart emoji?”

“Because that’s awkward and lame.”

“I’m awkward and lame. It’s fitting.”

Tiffany groaned. “At least use the heart eyes emoji.”

“I could do that.”

“Send her a damn-you-look-good gif.”

“That I can’t do.”

“Yes, you can.”

“Nope.”

Tiffany took my phone and began tapping on it quickly. “You’re making this harder than it needs to be.”

“What are you doing?” I reached for my phone.

She got up and walked away with my phone. “Helping you out.”

“Oh god.” I got up and had to chase her before she handed me my phone back. She sent both a damn gif and the heart eyes emoji. “Tiff…”

“No complaints. It’s done.”

“I can delete it.” I looked down at the message window and saw that Chantay was not only online but she just saw the message. I sat my phone face down on the counter. “She saw it.”

“Girls flirt and send compliments to other girls all the time. Relax. You can easily play it off if you need to. Although you shouldn’t need to because if she’s trying to see what’s up then you should let her know what is actually up.” Tiffany paused. “Does she like girls?”

“Fine time to ask that question.”

“My statement still stands but I’m curious now.”

“She was bisexual in college.”

“Did you have a crush on her in college?”

"Yes, but I was straight in college."

"Were you though?" Tiffany raised an eyebrow. "If you had a crush on her it stands to reason that you were likely not straight at all."

"I was only dating guys at the time."

"That's different."

I rolled my eyes.

"Have you come out to your line sisters?"

"Sort of."

"What does that mean?"

"Someone in the group chat asked me if I was dating anyone a few months ago and I said I had a girlfriend."

"How did they react?"

"Like I didn't say anything out of the ordinary. I didn't expect anyone to really react but they rolled like it was normal."

"It is normal."

"The only person who acted like it was a big deal was my mother and she just really wanted to be sure I was still willing to put in the work for her to have grandbabies."

Tiffany laughed. "Don't complain."

"I'm not. I'm thankful."

"You said she saw the message. Did she respond?"

I glanced at my phone without picking it up. "I don't know."

Tiffany sighed and picked up my phone. She handed it to me. “Unlock it.”

“No.”

“Why are you like this?” She put the phone in my hand. “Unlock the damn phone and see what she said.”

I huffed and unlocked my phone. I navigated back to the app and looked at my unread message. Her response made me smile.

Tiffany gently pushed me. “What did she say?”

“She sent me a wink emoji.”

“That’s it?”

“Yup.”

"Lawd she's just as lame and awkward as you are." Tiffany shook her head. Then she looked at me. "It gave you the warm and fuzzies, didn't it?"

I nodded.

"Are you going to respond?"

"Nope."

"What am I going to do with you?"

"Be my best friend and love me anyway." I gave her a hug.

"I guess." She laughed.

I was having an especially lonely moment and took a picture of myself in a sports bra and short shorts. It was also hot and I was waiting for maintenance to come and fix my broken AC. The picture was kind of sexy and I was feeling it so I posted it in my story. It was a bit too sexy for me to let it be up any longer than 24 hours. After an hour I had a message I refused to read from an ex-boyfriend I broke up with six years earlier. I swore he paid me more attention now than he did when we were together.

"Asshole." I mumbled under my breath as I started to close the app. Then a new message from Chantay popped up. I immediately clicked it to see that she sent me the heart eye emoji. Then she sent a flame emoji. Before I could think of a way to respond, she sent me a text message.

Chantay - Are you busy? Can you video chat?

Me - Sure. I'm not busy.

I leaned over and looked in the mirror across the room to make sure I still looked decent. My face was free of makeup and I had used a filter on that picture I posted. I still looked okay but really wished I looked better. It was too late to do anything about it. My phone started ringing with an incoming call a few seconds later.

I answered my phone and Chantay's face popped up on my screen. I smiled. "Hi."

"Hey." She smiled.

"What's up?"

"I tripped and fell in your thirst trap."

I laughed.

"You look hot."

"It is hot."

"That too."

I put her comment in the corner of my mind and decided to keep going like I didn't understand what she was saying. "My AC is broken. Currently waiting for maintenance to come and fix it."

"Hoping they get that shit fixed soon."

"Me too."

"So… I heard you were thinking about backing out of the girls' trip coming up."

I sighed. "Cause it isn't even a girls' trip anymore. Almost everyone is bringing their boyfriend or husband."

"I'm not bringing anybody."

"Anitra said you might."

"I'm not." She paused. "You should still come. We can hang out together when everyone gets boo'd up."

"How did this trip turn into a couple's trip?"

Chantay shrugged. “I think when Kelly’s husband complained that we just took a trip a couple of months ago.”

“That didn’t count. All of us weren’t there.”

“He doesn’t get it. He felt left out of the fun. Then he got the other guys involved and next thing you know they’re coming on the trip.”

I rolled my eyes. “I already canceled my hotel reservation.”

“Stay in my room with me.” She paused. “I still have a double from when I thought I was sharing a room with Taylor.”

The idea of sharing space with Chantay excited me but also freaked me out. “Are you sure?”

“Yes. It’ll be fun.” Chantay gave me these eyes that made me think she was fully prepared to beg me to go. “Please.”

I couldn’t tell her no. “Okay.”

“Great. It’s going to be a lot of fun. I promise.”

I bit my lip when she adjusted the phone and I saw she was wearing a tank top with straps that didn’t look like they were strong enough to contain her breasts. I wondered how I was going to survive a few days and nights in a hotel room with her. I needed to find extra willpower to bring with me. “Anitra said the guys were planning stuff to do together so that they weren’t hanging with us the whole time.”

“I mean they can come to the spa too. I don’t mind.”

I laughed. “Now you know Kelly’s husband ain’t setting foot in a spa.”

“Neither is Taylor’s boyfriend.” Chantay laughed.

“I hope they plan a lot of stuff because I don’t want to feel like the odd man out.”

“You won’t cause you’ll have me.” She paused. “We’re both single and can keep each other company.”

“I’m gonna hold you to that.” I heard a knock at my door. I sat my phone down and grabbed my shirt to put it on. “Maintenance is here.”

“I’ll stay on the phone with you. Those guys can be creepy.”

“Very creepy.” I took my phone and headed to go and answer my door.

“Maintenance. Here to fix your AC.” The guy said without really looking at me.

“Okay.” I let him in and he went straight over to the utility closet. I walked over to the living room and sat in the chair that was closest to the fan and open balcony door. It gave me a good view of the utility closet without needing to stand over him.

“They said it’s supposed to rain.” Chantay was walking around.

“I hope it rains here. Cool it off some.”

“I’m hoping we have good weather for the trip. Almanac says it should be good.”

“You checked an almanac?”

“Yes. I needed to start thinking about what I am going to pack.”

“I haven’t even thought about packing yet.”

Chantay laughed. “I obsess over what I’m going to wear.”

“I just pack whatever.”

“And you always end up looking like you spent a lot of time putting it together.” She shook her head.

“You act like you ever look bad.” I cut my eyes at her. “Whatever you pack, you’re going to look amazing.”

Chantay smiled. “I’m glad you think so.”

“I know so.”

Her smile got bigger. “What have you got going on this week?”

We talked for a long time about what we both had going on for the upcoming week. I couldn’t remember the two of us ever having a conversation for that long. We were on a line of seven girls. I couldn’t remember us ever being alone. The conversation flowed well and I found myself wondering what it would be like when we were alone at the hotel together. The maintenance guy fixed the AC and left quietly, simply waving on his way to the door, while we were talking.

"Girl, my phone is about to die."

"Mine probably is too."

"Is that repairman still there?"

"No. He left a bit ago."

"Did he fix the AC?"

"Yup. It's cooling off in here now."

"Good." Chantay paused and smiled at me. "I'm gonna let you go. We both need to charge our phones."

"Okay."

"I'll talk to you later."

I smiled. "Talk to you later."

After we hung up, I sat my phone next to me and sighed. I began to try and think of reasons to have another long conversation with Chantay before our trip.

After a mandatory morning meeting at work, I headed straight for the airport. By the time I arrived at the resort, my line sisters were all there. What I didn't expect was for them to all be in the hotel room I was sharing with Chantay. Anitra opened the door when I knocked. She took one of my bags and handed me a drink.

"Finally." She hollered.

Chantay came over to me. “We have the only room without a man in it.”

I nodded. “What are we drinking?”

“Rum and coke.” One of my line sisters called out.

Chantay looked at me. “You okay?”

“Yeah. Long day.”

“Drink your drink. Catch up to us. It’s time to relax.” Taylor came over and hugged me.

I took a healthy gulp of the drink to calm my nerves. I was really hoping to come to a quiet room and collect myself for a few before I got into the festivities with the girls. That clearly wasn’t going to happen.

“Why don’t you shower and change. We’re just drinking and then maybe going for a walk.” Chantay was still next to me after Taylor returned to the couch in our suite. “I figured you’d want the bed by the window.”

“Thanks.” I finished the drink and then took my bags over to my bed. I didn’t pay any attention to what the girls were talking about. I just grabbed some clothes to change into and my toiletry bag and headed to the bathroom. The first thing I noticed as I shut the bathroom door was the huge tub that was sitting next to a big shower. I wondered if Chantay told me the right amount when I asked her how much to send her to cover half the room. The suite was much more than I expected. I started the shower when I really just wanted to soak in the tub with a glass of wine.

When I came out of the bathroom, Dominique handed me a drink before she went in the bathroom. I dropped my clothes in my laundry bag and set it next to my suitcase. Then I joined my line sisters in the living area of the suite. They were complaining about their significant others so I just sipped my drink and nodded my head.

“What kind of shower gel do you use, Keya? That bathroom smells amazing.” Dominique stood in the doorway.

"I left it in the shower. I found it at an event I went to."

"Ooohh, there's a website." Dominique took a picture of the bottle with her phone. Then it got passed around the group. Once it made the rounds, she put it back in the bathroom.

I looked at Dominique as she sat on the floor next to me. "You on her website?"

"Yes. So many options."

"They all smell amazing. Her bar soap is wonderful too."

She groaned. "I'm going to get in trouble for shopping."

That set a few of my sorors off and the conversation went back to the guys. After a while, Anitra, the resident psychologist, shifted the conversation to more problem solving and less complaining. I was drinking my fourth drink, the last of what they brought when there was a knock at the suite door.

I took my drink with me to answer and laughed when I saw all the guys on the other side of the door. "Your gentlemen have come to collect you."

One by one my sorors left with their partners. Anitra was the last one to leave. She looked at me before I shut the door.

"Brunch tomorrow at eleven."

“Okay.” I waved as her husband took her arm and led her down the hall.

“Nobody is coming to get us.” Chantay was sitting on the couch when I shut the door.

I finished my drink. “You want me to go out and knock to come and get you.”

She smiled. “You’re sweet.”

I sat down on the other end of the couch. “Don’t want to deny you from feeling what the others felt.”

Chantay and I held eye contact for a few moments. Then she leaned over and crawled across the couch until she was right in front of me. My breath got caught in my throat and my heart began to race. She moved in closer and had me pinned to the corner of the couch while she hovered over me. I wanted her to kiss me so badly that I closed my eyes. As soon as her lips touched mine, my heart stopped for a moment and I thought I might pass out. It took me a second but I was able to pull myself together and kiss her back.

Chantay pulled back and got up off the couch. She reached her hand out to me. "Come to bed with me."

I took her hand and let her lead me back to the bedroom of the suite. She sat down on the bed and pulled me in between her legs. We both took our shirts off. I reached behind her and unhooked her bra while her hands gravitated to my breasts.

"So perfect." She mumbled before putting one of my breasts in her mouth. Her hands slipped down in my shorts. I unbuttoned them and she pushed them down. "You have the perfect body."

"If you don't stand your gorgeous ass up and take off the rest of your clothes."

Chantay stood up and kissed me. I pushed her leggings down over her hips and off her ass. Chantay had amazing curves and I couldn't help but run my hands up and down them.

"How's your focus?"

Her question confused me at first. Then she got on the bed and I realized what she was proposing. She laid back on the bed and I got on top, hovering over her with my head just above where her legs met. I was so anxious that I gave a quick kiss to each of her thighs before burying my face in her pussy. She tasted so good and I got lost in what I was doing until she pulled me down on her face and started doing the same. Then I wondered how good my focus actually was. Chantay was very good with her lips and tongue and I did my best to give just as good as I was getting.

When her orgasm hit, I felt like I won the race. I did have a head start. I got to enjoy the taste of her climax while she moaned into my thigh. It didn't take her long to get herself together and focus her tongue on pulling my orgasm out of me. I came hard and rolled off of her so I didn't squeeze her head between my thighs. Chantay rolled with me and held my legs open while she finished. Then we both laid on our backs and caught our breath.

She sat up. "You're a squirter."

"And you're a gusher." I slowly ran my fingers up her side.

"That was wonderful."

"It was." I finally looked at her face. She smiled at me. "Now what?"

"We turn on the television and you let me hold you while we go to sleep. It'll be time for brunch before we know it."

I smiled and sat up. "Okay."

Chantay grabbed the remote and turned on the television. I got up and adjusted the AC in the room. We both tied our hair up and then got under the covers of her bed. She held me in her arms and kissed the back of my neck. Her breasts felt good against my back.

I started to wonder what was going to happen next for us. "Tay."

"Huh?"

"What is going..."

"Shhhh." She kissed me on the back of my neck again. "Don't think. There'll be plenty of time to think tomorrow. Let's not do it tonight."

I sighed. "Okay."

“TV and sleep.” She gently squeezed me.

“TV and sleep.” I repeated.

I woke up to Chantay sitting on the edge of the bed, rubbing my arm. She smiled at me when I opened my eyes. I smiled back, then rolled over and pulled the covers over my head.

She laughed. “Keya, we gotta get up for brunch. They’ll come looking for us if we don’t show.”

I groaned and moved the covers. “I need to sleep off that rum. We aren’t twenty anymore.”

“Just chase it with some mimosa. You’ll be fine.”

I sat up and looked at her. “How is that a good idea?”

She shrugged.

I frowned. “I need to brush my teeth.”

“That sounds like you’re getting up to me.”

I cut my eyes at her before I got out of bed and headed into the bathroom. After emptying my bladder, I washed my hands and brushed my teeth. I decided to wash my face while in the shower. As much as I wanted to go and crawl back into the bed, I knew Chantay was right. My sorors would come looking for me.

When I came out of the bathroom in a towel, Chantay was still in her underwear. She was holding up a dress in one hand and a shirt in the other.

“What are we doing today?”

“Brunch and exploring.”

“The shirt and shorts.” I sat on the bed with my lotion. “You know Kelly and Anitra are going to want to zipline.”

“They’ve only been talking about it since we started planning this trip.”

“Exactly.” I started to lotion my body. As I did, I couldn’t help but watch her get dressed.

“What are you going to wear?”

"Capris and a top."

Chantay nodded. She didn't look at me. She grabbed her makeup bag and went over to the mirror. Feeling slightly awkward, I went over to my suitcase and started to get dressed. I felt like she was watching me but I didn't dare look to see. My mind was racing trying to figure out how things would be between us now. We weren't that close before but I definitely wanted to be closer now. I just worried that she might not feel the same way.

When I thought I might have the nerve to say something, there was a knock at our suite door. Chantay turned and looked at the clock. She looked at me and rolled her eyes before smiling. I laughed and finished fixing my shirt while she went to answer the door. I heard several of my sorors walk into the room. I walked to the doorway to see exactly who it was.

Anitra came over to me while Dominique and Kelly sat on the couch. I took my scarf off while looking at Anitra.

"We were coming."

"I know. We decided to head over together. Everyone else is downstairs." She glanced in the bedroom. "Did you even sleep in your bed?"

Panic took over me for a brief moment before I pulled myself together. "I passed out on top of the covers."

Chantay briefly glanced at me as she slipped past us. "Let me grab my purse."

"I just want to fix my face real quick and I'll be ready." I went into the bedroom and dropped my scarf in my suitcase. Anitra and Chantay headed back out into the living space of the suite while I did my makeup. It didn't take me long to add a little color to my eyes and lips.

Chantay came to the doorway.

Anitra yelled from the living room. "Tell her she looks gorgeous so we can go."

Chantay smiled. "You look gorgeous."

"Thank you." I smiled at her before grabbing my lipstick and turning to get my purse. Then I followed her out of the bedroom, trying not to stare at her ass.

"Okay. I'm ready."

We all stayed at brunch so long the waitress helping us had to find a nice way to ask us to leave. She was so sweet about it and we made sure to leave her a nice tip. I lost count of how many pitchers of mimosa we went through. There were twelve of us in the group. We were sitting at a table and Chantay was at the opposite end from me. Every so often I would glance in her direction. We made eye contact a few times but for the most part, I stayed focused on whatever the topic of discussion happened to be on my end of the table.

After brunch, we went to the zipline. Chantay ended up being my partner by default. We didn't have a moment alone for most of the day. We just shared occasional glances. There was a long one while we both got strapped up to go on the zipline. I had done it before but was still very nervous. She reached out and held my hand for a few moments before we were both launched down the zipline.

When we got to the other side and unhooked, Chantay held both of my hands. "You good?"

I nodded as I caught my breath.

“You survived.”

“Barely.”

She laughed. She let my hand go when the attendants came over to help us out of the gear. We met up with the others once we had all the gear off. There was one more couple after us. Once we were all done, we headed to go eat. Chantay was once again at the other end of the table. I wished she was sitting next to me but I knew if she was then I would want to touch her. Luckily our sorors and their significant others were enough of a distraction. I didn’t get lost in my head until we were heading back to our room. Then I was overwhelmed with what was going to happen next.

Chantay and I didn't say a word to each other as we walked down the hall from the elevator to our room. I went straight to the bathroom when we got inside. When I came out, she went in. I sat down on my bed and tried to figure out what I was going to say to her. So many things were running through my mind but I didn't feel like I could articulate any of it.

Chantay came out of the bathroom and I noticed that the water was running. She grabbed something from her bag and went back into the bathroom. After a moment, she came and stood in the doorway. She looked at me while pulling her braids up in a ponytail. "Come take a bath with me."

As I stood up, she took her shirt off. We got undressed and I followed her into the bathroom. She turned the water off. The tub was full and it looked like she dropped a bath bomb in it. The whole bathroom smelled wonderful. We climbed into the tub and sat down in the hot water. It felt so good. Our legs intertwined as we got comfortable.

Chantay pulled me close. “I’ve been dying to kiss you all day.”

I leaned closer and kissed her softly. “Same.”

“I want to be close to you but if I sit next to you I’m gonna want to touch you and then someone will see and we’ll have to explain something that I don't know if we're ready to explain."

I smiled and kissed her again. She was saying everything that had been on my mind. "It's new."

"And still a bit complicated."

"Exactly."

Chantay pulled me so that we were pressed against each other. My clit throbbed wanting even more pressure. Chantay kissed me. "I want this to be about more than sex but I also want desperately for you to make me cum."

She kissed me on my neck and I traced my fingers down her back. I rocked my hips to increase the pressure between us.

Chantay met my pressure with some of her own and I moaned. We both leaned back against the tub and found the perfect angle. She held my hand over the edge of the tub and we found a delicious rhythm together. Between that and the temperature and fragrance of the water, I was in heaven.

Chantay squeezed my hand and picked up her pace which let me know she was close, while also pushing me closer to the edge. I matched her pace and my orgasm arrived faster than I had anticipated. Chantay reached underwater with her other hand and squeezed my thigh.

"You okay?" I asked before I even caught my breath.

“That was so necessary.” Chantay spoke softly.

We sat for a few minutes without saying anything, still holding hands with her other hand now just resting on my thigh.

Finally, Chantay sat up. “I need to wash the bath off me.”

I couldn’t help but laugh.

“What? Is that weird?”

“No.” I shook my head. “At least I don’t think so. I do the same thing.”

We got up and got out of the tub. Chantay let the water out of the tub while I started the shower. After a quick shower together, we went into the bedroom. I pulled on a pair of panties and an extra-long tank top that I liked to sleep in. She put on panties and a t-shirt.

“My bed again?” She asked.

I nodded while tying my scarf and then we got into bed. This time I held her in my arms. “Should we talk?”

“I don’t know what to say.”

“Me either.”

“So, let’s just go to sleep and figure it out tomorrow.”

“Okay.”

We didn’t figure it out the next day, or the day after that. Instead, we spent most of our time enjoying our vacation with our line sisters. It wasn't so bad being around all the couples. Especially since we would go back to our room at night and spend a good amount of time giving each other orgasms. It was the best vacation I had in a long time.

So naturally, I was depressed on our last night there. We had a ton to drink at dinner and I was quiet as we headed back to our room. Anitra's husband insisted that they both walk us back to make sure we were okay. I was quietly walking while the three of them were talking.

Chantay slowed down to walk next to me as we were walking down the hallway to our suite. "You okay?"

I nodded.

Anitra walked backward, looking at us. “You two are cute together. That should be a thing.”

“Anitra.” Her husband tried to hush her when my eyes got wide.

“Don’t make that face Keya. I’ve known you both since forever. You are exactly each other’s type.”

“Baby, leave them alone.” He stopped her as she almost walked past our suite door.

“It’s been on my mind and I’m speaking my mind.” Anitra rolled her eyes at him.

Chantay looked like she wanted to burst out laughing but she held it in.

Anitra looked at her. “Tay, remember you used to have a crush on her.”

“I told you that fifteen years ago.” Chantay shook her head. “How do you remember that?”

“I remember everything.” Anitra smiled.

“I’m going to take her away now.” Her husband took her by the arm and started to lead her down the hall.

“I think it’s a great idea. I’m sure everyone in the line will agree.”

“Thanks for your blessing.” Chantay waved.

“Love you guys.” Anitra waved as her husband led her to the elevator.

“Love you too.” Chantay and I responded at the same time. Her husband stood at the end of the hallway while we opened our door. We went inside.

I turned to her quickly. “I’m going to shower.”

“Okay.” She replied as I had already turned and headed to the bathroom.

While I was in the shower, I made an attempt to figure out my life. Unfortunately, I was still too drunk and my thoughts were all over the place. The one thing I kept settling back on was that I wanted to spend more time with Chantay. I got out of the shower and sat on my bed wrapped in a towel. Chantay went into the bathroom after me. While I lotioned my body, I tried to figure out how we could just stay on vacation forever.

When the shower stopped, it seemed like all my thoughts seemed to come together. As soon as Chantay came out of the bathroom my mouth started going.

“I really think that we should give us a chance. I know you’re an hour from me but I think we should try. I want to talk to you all the time and I want to see you as much as possible.”

Chantay sat down on the bed next to me. “Okay.”

I was quiet for a moment while she started putting lotion on. My brain was very slow processing what she said. "Okay?"

"Yeah." She smiled at me. "I want that too. I'm not even nervous about our friendship because we've been friends for years. As long as we don't lose sight of that I think we'll be fine."

"So, we're going to do this?"

"Yes."

"Can we not tell the group just yet. I want to enjoy us for a bit without their input."

Chantay smiled. "Sure. Anitra isn't even going to remember what she said tonight."

"She really won't."

We laughed. Chantay leaned over and kissed me. "Wait. I gotta tell Taylor. She's my best friend. She won't tell the others."

"Okay."

"So, we go home tomorrow. How soon before I see you again?"

I thought for a second. "I could just go home with you."

She laughed. "You have work."

"Oh." I frowned. "I wish I worked from home full time and not just part-time."

"Next weekend?"

"Yes."

“How about a couple orgasms to tie us over?”

I smiled at her. “That sounds like a wonderful idea.”

The Friday evening after vacation, I was sitting in traffic on my way to Chantay’s townhouse. I hadn’t been there since her housewarming five years earlier. The whole way there I kept praying our chemistry wasn’t a vacation phenomenon. We started texting each other right after we got back. It was nice to talk to each other outside of the group chat. There were a few video calls as well. I usually hated those kinds of calls but it was different looking at Chantay's face on the other end. I thought about her all day while I was supposed to be working and I was cursing at traffic for keeping me from her.

Just as I was cursing at the traffic in front of me, she called me. I answered with a forced smile. "Hello."

"Hey." She paused. "Why do you sound like you are forcing a smile or clenching your teeth?"

I laughed. "I'm in traffic."

"So, you didn't get lost?"

"No. I'm like twenty minutes away if the traffic gods have pity on me."

“Okay. I was just checking. Take deep breaths.”

“I’m trying.”

“Do you still want to go out?”

“I’m dressed to go out. I just don’t want to drive anymore.”

“Just finish driving to my house and I’ll take over from there. We’ll go out and have a drink or two.”

I groaned at the traffic stopping in front of me. “I should get off the phone. I need to curse some more before I get to you.”

Chantay laughed. “Okay. See you in a few.”

“Hopefully.” I hung up and immediately started cursing at traffic again.

Thirty minutes later, Chantay opened her garage as I pulled up in the driveway. She came out and met me after I parked. I shut the car door after I got out and she immediately started giving me kisses.

“Thank you for braving traffic to see me.” She said between kisses.

I couldn’t help but giggle. “You’re welcome.”

“You look gorgeous.” Chantay took a step back.

I looked down at my tight black pants and loose tank top. Then I looked at Chantay, wearing a purple sundress that was hitting all of her curves. “Thank you. You look great.”

“Thanks. Let’s go put your bag in the house and then I’ll order a car so we can go out.”

“I could use a drink after that drive.” I followed her inside the house.

“We can go someplace just the two of us or we can go meet up with some of my friends.”

“Whatever you want to do is fine with me.”

“There’ll be a live band where friends are.”

“That sounds good.”

I dropped my bag in Chantay's bedroom, went to the bathroom, and then met her down in the living room. A few minutes later, we were in the back of a car headed into the city. We met up with a few of her friends at a nice lounge. It was nice being out and being open with our affection. Chantay kept her hand on my thigh for most of the night. Her friends were great and the band was awesome. The drinks were also very good and we had quite a few of them. I was glad we didn't have to worry about driving home.

We were both scrolling through our phones on the way home. Chantay reached over and showed me a picture of the two of us that one of her friends took shortly after we met up with them.

"We look good together."

"We do." I smiled.

"I'll send it to you." She glanced up at me. "We should take more pictures together."

"Planning a photo shoot in your mind?"

She laughed. "Maybe."

"Okay."

"I like this."

"What?"

"Going out with you but also knowing we'll be staying in for the rest of the weekend."

"Staying in sounds lovely."

"Can we do this every weekend?"

"What? Go out and get drunk with friends?"

"See each other."

"Oh." I smiled. "Yes."

Chantay leaned over and kissed me. "Good."

Before I knew it, three months had passed. Since I worked from home on Mondays and Fridays, I would drive down to stay with Chantay on Thursday night and just work from her house. I'd go home on

Monday night. Once a month she would come up to stay with me at my place for the weekend. She hated driving more than I did and she also didn't like that it meant we only saw each other from Friday night to Sunday night on those weekends. She was spoiled with the time I could give her on my weekends and I didn't mind spoiling her.

We didn't say anything to our line sisters about us dating for most of that time. The only one who knew was Taylor. Then we got heavy into preparing for Dominique's wedding and the group started pressing Chantay and I to find out who we were bringing as a date. Our sorors got relentless because neither of us had spoken about our love life since before our vacation.

Finally, while we were sitting together with our legs intertwined on her couch reading separate books, Chantay cracked and told the group chat.

Chantay - So I'm bringing Keya and she is bringing me because we are dating and I hope it is cool with y'all because I am ridiculously happy.

I saw her type the message. I heard my phone vibrate when she sent the message. I just didn't look at the message for another twenty minutes because I was caught up in the story I was reading. By the time I got to it several of our sorors had replied with applause and hearts. I sat my phone down, crawled over to Chantay, and kissed her.

"Ridiculously happy?"

"Yes."

"Me too."

She smiled. "Good."

I went back to my seat. "One more chapter and I'm going to start dinner."

"Two more chapters and I'll join you." She rubbed my leg and went back to reading her book.

“Okay. I have something to tell you.” Tiffany picked up her drink just after the waitress sat it in front of her.

We thanked the waitress and then I looked at my best friend. “What’s up?”

“I got that job I interviewed for.”

“Congratulations.” We toasted our glasses.

“That means I’ll be moving closer to DC as soon as possible.” She paused. “But we’ll still see each other because you are almost always in Alexandria with Chantay.”

I smiled. “I applied to go fully remote with my position. The position is based in DC.”

"Oh wow. Things are going that well with Chantay?"

"She's been hinting about me moving in with her and wishing I didn't have to work three days in Baltimore." I paused. "I wonder if we're moving too fast."

"Too fast?" Tiffany raised her eyebrows. "You two have known each other since college. That was like fifteen years ago."

"Over fifteen years." I mumbled in response.

"Exactly. I don't think y'all are moving too fast." Tiffany paused. "When is your lease up? You moved before I did and mine is up in three months."

“I have to give them an answer in a week.”

“So, tell them you’re moving out and pack.”

“But what if I don’t get the remote position?”

“Don’t even talk like that. That job is yours. Own it.” Tiffany smiled at me. “Have you talked to Chantay about this?”

“Not really. I told her about my lease being up and then she really started hinting at me moving in with her. I didn’t say anything about the job.”

“Talk to her. I bet she says the same thing I’m saying.”

“Y’all always agree anyway.” I rolled my eyes.

“That’s because she’s my buddy.” Tiffany laughed. “Y’all have the wedding this weekend?”

“Yeah. We fly out tomorrow.”

“Make sure y’all talk. If you care about her like I know you care about her then you need to include her in your future planning.”

“You’re right.”

“I know.” Tiffany smiled and then sipped her drink.

Chantay and I were sitting at the bridal party table, resting after a long stretch of dancing to celebrate Dominique's wedding. I couldn't help but stare at her while she chatted with Renae, one of our sorors. Her hand was resting on the part of my thigh revealed by the split in my bridesmaids' dress. It had been so wonderful to be able to show her affection in front of our sorors and it not be a big deal. They were all super supportive of our relationship while also not making it a big deal. The group chat went on as it always had.

The DJ called the single ladies to the dance floor for the throwing of the bouquet.

Chantay looked at me. "You're not going either?"

"I'm not single."

"I know that's right." She laughed. "I don't want to give Anitra any ideas."

"Come on, you know she's already planning y'all wedding." Renae said as she got up.

"I don't know that I'm ready for all that." I sipped my drink.

"We're taking things one step at a time. I gotta get you to move in with me first." Chantay looked at me as Renae walked away.

"I was going to tell you later but I heard back about a position I applied for."

"What kind of position?"

"A slight promotion and fully remote in my department but my main office would move to DC."

Chantay's eyes got wide. "And? You got it?"

"Yeah."

She squealed and gave me a hug. "Oh my god. How long ago did you apply? Why didn't you say anything? This is awesome. It's a promotion, right? Does this mean you are going to move with me?"

I looked into her wide eyes and realized how much I loved her. "Do I have to answer all of that?"

"Yes."

I smiled. “I applied two weeks ago but it was only posted internally. No one else applied for it. I found out Thursday when I checked in before we headed for the airport. It’s a slight promotion.”

“That’s still great.”

“And yes, I’ll move in with you.”

She squealed again. Then she leaned over and kissed me. “I’ll share my closet with you.”

“I’m fine with taking the closet in the second bedroom.”

“We can turn that room into your office or the loft can be your office and the room can be your dressing room. We can make room for your furniture. I can get rid of some stuff."

Chantay kept talking and I sat there in awe for a moment. Then I waited for her to take a breath and I kissed her. We smiled at each other when I pulled back from the kiss.

"Calm down."

She took a deep breath. "I really love you and want to be with you as often as possible."

I kissed her. "I love you too."

"Okay you two. Enough of the lovey dovey shit. Come dance with us." Dominique stood on the other side of the table with her hand on her hip.

"Yes ma'am." Chantay responded as I laughed. I couldn't help but admire her curves as she stood up. All the bridesmaids were wearing the same color, lavender, but we each had a different style of dress. Chantay was wearing the hell out of her dress. She looked at me and held out her hand. "Stop looking at my ass and come dance."

I took her hand and followed her to the dance floor.

~the end~

Other works by Turtleberry

Are You Okay?

Nobody's Somebody

Sweet Turtleberry Jam Volume One

These Women Book One

These Women Book Two

These Women Book Three

Happily Ever After

Sweet Turtleberry Jam Volume Two

Catching Evie

Needs To Be Met

Love Unexpected

Lena's Chance At Love

Both Sides Of Me

Whiskey Kisses

Halloween Spice

It For Me

Days of Summer

One More Kiss

The Friend

Finding Love

My Neighbor

On Break

Living The Dream

www.sweetturtleberry.com

www.ingramcontent.com/pod-product-compliance
Lightning Source LLC
LaVergne TN
LVHW050336160826
845677LV00014B/3631

* 9 7 9 8 8 4 8 8 1 5 4 7 4 *